For both Leroy and Ruby, life assaults have crushed their original dreams forcing them to aimlessly navigate the New York City streets year after year. The unfamiliar and unforgiving pavement of Harlem was gobbling up their dreams. The survival game was their goal.

EGGPLANT
Man

MARGO DE LEAVER

ARCHWAY
PUBLISHING

Credits: International Society of Poets Outstanding achievement in Poetry Award 2006

Archway Publishing books may be ordered through booksellers or by contacting:

Archway Publishing
1663 Liberty Drive
Bloomington, IN 47403
www.archwaypublishing.com
1 (888) 242-5904

ISBN: 978-1-4808-4163-5 (sc)
ISBN: 978-1-4808-4164-2 (e)

Library of Congress Control Number: 2016920925

Print information available on the last page.

Archway Publishing rev. date: 08/18/2018

ACKNOWLEDGEMENTS

Profound Appreciation and Gratitude to:

My editor, Brenda Roberts, for her selfless and knowledgeable dedication to detail with a loving heart

My deceased parents, Bill and Syl, for their silent eternal support and love

My daughter, Chloe Russell, who always loved me through it all, and encouraged me to keep moving forward, despite any setbacks

My three sisters, Michele Balamani, Cheryl De Leaver, and Donna De Leaver, who were always so supportive of all of my writings and encouraged me to continue writing this book to the finish line

Souleymane Drame, who kept reminding me to work on my story and was so supportive when I needed that boost

Michel Doidic, who consistently reminded me to keeping writing: from the beginning, he read every chapter I sent him, and even put a floating message on my computer screen, reminding me to write another chapter

All of my friends who honored me by taking the time to promptly read my initial rough copy and to get back to me with such support and good wishes (Jennifer Campbell, Gerry Russell, Jelani Russell, Mary Flaherty, Sum-Yee Wang, Michele Doidic, Karen Bailey, Aunty Ag)

A Special Thank You to Everyone who supports me by taking a chance, who purchases and reads this book. I would love to hear from you! margo@margodeleaver.com, website www.margodeleaver.com

To my Mother, Sylvia De Leaver, who remained an avid reader into her nineties and taught me the love of books

To my Father, William De Leaver, who was my hero and always loved me

COMMENTS PAGE

There is a special **sweetness that** is exclusive to love born in unlikely places. Eggplant man is a no turning back journey into the speck of light that never died in the dark nights of two war torn souls. Congratulations to **Margo De Leaver** who captured it all, like she was there.

Dr. Michele Balamani Silvera

Psychotherapist, crisis counselor, writer, pastor Upper Marlboro, Maryland

"I'm an enthusiastic fan of Margo De Leaver's skills, especially in literature. She writes with her guts, and with her heart! Her book made me thrilled. Congratulations, Margo, and please don't give up!

Michèle Doidic, a French books lover, avid reader, teacher, presently living in Paris, France

"Eggplant Man" captures the struggle of life on the streets and the small victories of human kindness. Hooray to new author Margo De Leaver...."

Mary Flaherty, Women's Healthcare Advocate, Philanthropist, Dog Lover and rescuer, avid reader and traveler Los Angeles

Eggplant man is an imploding manifestation of an embracing life assault, a realistic portrayal of circumstance visually sustained in an inescapable series of events wherein the characters become one with the reader! As I read the book there were times when I became lost among the characters and I was an active part of the plot as it unfolded. I am the nemesis I am the plot and I am the inference and the conclusion. Well done!

Cheryl De Leaver, Teacher, poet, actor, painter NYC native

"Eggplant man is a creative and exciting adventure that takes you through the lives of two seemingly different characters. It keeps you turning the page while discovering the unique connection that the two main characters share. Great read!"

Chloe Russell Stanford University - Psychology Doctoral Student, teacher, Los Angeles native, yoga instructor, dog lover, beach lover, avid theater goer, crazy about NYC presently living in San Francisco

Through the story of Eggplant Man, Margo De Leaver, shows us that love has no boundaries, no color, no social class, it just works its miracle anywhere it lands. Read on, and your view on the extent of its reach will be enhanced.

Michel Doidic Digital Music Programmer, writer, animator, true scientist, France native presently living in Westlake Village, California

Eggplant Man is an outstanding must read that keeps you captivated until the end!

Gerald Russell Retired Hospital Administrator, Avid Movie and Theater Goer, world traveler, skiing enthusiast, Buffalo, NY native, now residing in Los Angeles

A gripping page-turner about a homeless man's daily struggles to survive, to find love, and even happiness. A story that is representative of the growing population of the homeless in our society today.

Karen Bailey Naturopath, teacher, avid reader, native New Yorker

"Eggplant man is a creative and exciting adventure that takes you through the lives of two seemingly different characters. It keeps you turning the page while discovering the unique connection that the two main characters share. Complex and interesting character development. Great read!"

Donna Ocasio Psychotherapist, animal lover, avid movie goer The Bronx, New York

A raw, intense experience. Vividly descriptive...get ready to be transported!

Jelani Russell Avid reader and movie goer, animal lover Los Angeles native

"Love may be unfathomable, but exploring its depths with Ruby and the Eggplant Man is a journey well worth the taking." —Brenda C. Roberts

CHAPTER 1

Garbage Day

RUBY

It was August 2005 in Harlem, one of those damp, hot and heavy days that made your skin glisten with sweat and oil. No matter how many showers you took, you felt wet and sticky. It was a bad hair day, making permanents droop, naturals shrink, and nylon panties wedge up and stick to your butt. By noon on this particular Monday, the air was so thick that breathing became a conscious endeavor, like sucking air through cotton.

Ruby constantly mumbled to herself about the items she had salvaged from other people's trash on her routine afternoon treasure hunts. Today was garbage day, and she had only two hours left to complete her tour. The ominous looking scar on her left cheek hinted at a past she wanted to forget. It changed shapes, contorting her face as she squinted in the beaming sunlight.

She stood just short of five feet but appeared much taller.

Her sepia-colored face was dotted with those tiny brown mole intrusions that one hopes never to inherit. Oversized multi-stained khaki pants and a torn white cotton tee shirt were stark contrasts to her meticulously well-groomed hair. Ruby always kept her hair neatly plaited in two symmetrical rows, which gleamed blue-black in the merciless rays of the high noon sun.

Rarely looking directly at anyone or anything, Ruby's hazel eyes darted nervously from one point to the next, focusing only momentarily on anything that caught her attention.

Out of the corner of her eye, she caught a glimpse of a familiar figure. He was propped up against the graffiti covered wall of Bubba's barber shop and shoe shine parlor. Bubba was long gone, and now an Asian owner stood in the doorway. Mr. Wong had been the proprietor for the past six years. He always wore a grimace of dissatisfaction on his face. Perhaps he regretted being in a place so distant from his Taiwan origin.

Ruby's eyes came to rest upon the half-reclining man. He appeared to be holding up the shop's wall, rather than vice versa. "Atlas in black", she thought, "with the weight of the world on his back." She stared much longer than usual. Something about him was holding her attention.

He wore a tattered three-piece navy suit, exposing his calloused gray knees and elbows. His wine-stained striped tie was loosened at the neck and hung like an albatross noose, weighted and threatening. Ruby was searching to find what it was about this man that was drawing her interest. Perhaps it was his torn, once white, now muddy beige shirt, which revealed a contrasting triangular area of ebony skin at the jugular notch? His matted, wiry hair, was infiltrated with coiled silver and black strands. His mane stood four inches above his scalp like a crown.

"He was king of what," Ruby mumbled to herself. Then, as if someone had heard her mute query, she heard a whisper, "It's his skin, Ruby."

Yes, his captivating skin tone held her, mesmerized her. It shone purple-black in the sunlight. A fine layer of oil rested on its surface and gleamed like polished onyx, ultra-smooth and unblemished.

It reminded Ruby of something she had recently come across in her rummages. She frantically began to re-search the last three garbage cans she had visited. Ruby was disappointed that the first two cans did not reveal the item she quested.

It sat on the bottom of the third can. Ruby was delighted. She picked up the refuse as if it were a valuable gem. The large piece of eggplant skin, purple-black, smooth and shiny, rested in her palm.

Ruby smiled, her deep dimples taking their rightful place on her cheeks. The lower point of the C-shaped scar on her left cheek just touched the top of her left dimple. It rested there, like a scythe threatening to remove the dimple. As she smiled, the scar seemed to soften, perhaps changing its mind to inflict further damage. Ruby continued forward in the direction of the seated man.

CHAPTER 2

Naming Day

Gently holding the vegetable skin in her left hand, Ruby began to walk towards the figure against the wall. Her gait was like that of an ant, carefully checking out the territory in front of her, crossing the sidewalk in staccato movements.

The half-reclining man saw her coming. He rapidly finished off the chocolate bar he was eating and started to sit up. She was only about fifty feet from him now, but she seemed to take a long time to reach her destination.

Not sure of her intentions, he raised himself to a more defiant sitting position. His hair already stood rebelliously on his head, resistant to any idea of lying down. It was like a corona of tall close-fitting coils matted together in unity. The whites of his dark eyes, now bourbon brown, were reminders of his past journeys into liquid abuse. ("…dark eyes, whenever I think of you…I think dark eyes")

The sclera were like dark yellow crescent moons engulfing desolate black irises.

As Ruby got closer, she noticed the man's high, angular cheekbones and flaring black nostrils. His powerful nares knew a history of past indulgences he could no longer afford.

"Sniffing white snow through quivering black nostrils
Going home but ain't nobody there
Meeting up with a group of white hostiles
Being identified by the style of your hair"

While waiting for Ruby, the dark man noticed a perfectly smooth, shiny mahogany roach ease out from under the parlor. It was obviously a survivor, confident in its approach. Without hesitation, he formed a hammer-shaped fist and came down mercilessly on his victim; a hot and heavy ending to its life. This was a futile act of retribution on the innocent arthropod. It reminded him of the Selma judge's mallet that wrongly sentenced him to 15 to years of hard labor. He also was innocent.

"Squashing that roach who thought he got away
Smoking that roach from the other day"

When Ruby reached him, their eyes met for a moment. Almost imperceptibly, he nodded his head indicating it was fine for her to proceed. For the second time that day, she allowed her eyes to focus. Her nystagmus paused as she gave her attention to the interesting person in front of her. Ruby noted his attire. She was curious as to why he was dressed that way. Ruby had glanced at him several times before from a distance, while making her daily garbage runs. He was always sitting in front of the barber shop, but Ruby had not taken much notice of him.

Ruby was unaware that the man had worn that outfit daily, like a uniform, for the past 15 years. After journeying from Alabama, he had finally arrived in New York City, in search of a new beginning. He was dressed in his best attire, in the only suit he owned. He spent months looking for gigs or any work in the City. With one job rejection after another and no place to go, he and his banjo had remained on the streets of Harlem. Odd jobs here and there, and his banjo, kept him alive. He could not bring himself to remove the suit, which had been a gift from his deceased mother. That suit and his banjo were his only connection to what had been.

Ruby read his nod as a silent permit to proceed. Was that kindness, fatigue or sadness she saw in his eyes? It did not matter to Ruby in that moment. There was something she needed to do. Without hesitation, Ruby continued approaching the sitting figure.

When she was about twelve inches away, she knelt in front of him and looked directly into his eyes. She remembered her mother's words: "When you got somethin' important to say to someone, Baby, you needs to look them in the eyes, so they knows it's true." Her reply to her mother was always the same: "Yes, Ma'Dear."

The banjo player felt uncomfortable with the closeness of Ruby. The distinct smell of coconut oil, which hung in the humid, damp heat of Harlem's summer, was dizzying. Then he saw it. How could he have ever missed it? He was captivated by the dancing scar protruding from her left cheek. It was in motion, synchronized with Ruby's facial movements. Only her hazel eyes were still.

His discomfort quickly dissipated as a memory began to emerge. The scar was familiar, and for anyone who lived in Metairie, Louisiana, in the early seventies, the story was unforgettable.

Before Ruby realized what was happening, the man with those dark ebony eyes slowly reached up and began to gently stroke the keloid growth embedded in her cheek. She glanced down at his hand. His broad, ashy fingers, marfanoid in length, had nails the color of brown sugar.

Ruby felt the roughness of a calloused fingertip coursing the length of her C shaped facial member. His touch seemed to discern the secret of her blemish, exposing the memory it held inside. An almost healing warmth emanated from his fingertip. Ruby felt a tingling sensation come alive in the lesion. The scar calmed down and acquiesced to his touch. It promptly halted its gyrations, as if obeying a silent command.

CHAPTER 3
Game Changer

With the rough feeling of the finger on her scar, Ruby thought she smelled cloves and was momentarily distracted. Her mind took her back to a fateful day almost 20 years earlier. It was Christmas Eve. Her husband, Harold, many years her senior, had returned home from work, drunk as usual. Ruby was preparing a ham for Christmas dinner. She had just finished putting the nail-shaped aromatic cloves into the many cross-sections on the fatty surface of the meat.

"They god-damned fired my ass today, little-girl," said Harold in a burst of rage. "Said I was drunk." Ruby hated being called little-girl, hated having a drunken husband twice her age, and hated thinking about the inevitable consequences of having an unemployed husband in the poor South.

The words uncontrollably flew out of her mouth. "Harold,

you are drunk, you are always drunk. I'm surprised it took them so long to get rid of your behind!"

In a moment of insanity and drunken anger, Harold picked up a paring knife and made a huge gaping slit in Ruby's left cheek. She felt numb all over, floating in a cloudy weightlessness. A thick, warm liquid ran down her cheek and into her open mouth. It tasted salty. "Am I crying?" she wondered. "Are those tears I taste?" She looked at her apron and noticed the bright red stains intermixing with the daffodil landscape pattern of her smock.

Two phrases flowed into her head. "Don't never let no man hurt you, Baby. He do it once, he do it again," Ma'Dear always said. Even her long-gone Daddy, who left before she turned twelve, had put in his two cents. "If a man ever hits you, he's dead, baby-girl! If you don't do it, I will," he had said.

In her shock and fear, Ruby grabbed the nearby carving knife and plunged it deeply into Harold's chest, sending him swiftly back to the dust from which he came. Although it was considered self-defense by the law, it was all over the papers. After that incident, wherever she went in Metairie, people would whisper and stare. Ruby came north to Harlem, New York, trying to escape her notoriety in her home town. She wanted a new start in a big city where she could become anonymous.

She moved in with her mother's half-sister, Aunt Peggy, and found a part-time job waitressing at a small coffee shop on St. Nicholas Avenue near 135th Street. Aunt Peggy, noticing her husband's attentions to her niece, soon became jealous of Ruby. She began accusing the girl of flirting with her husband. After trying to avoid the husband's daily sexual advances, Ruby knew she had to leave Aunt Peggy's place.

Desperate, she rented a vermin-infested room on 115th Street. Her savings were meager and her part-time salary insufficient. Each day, Ruby had to step over drug addicts and the homeless sleeping on the steps and in the lobby of her six-story walk-up. Soon, Ruby experienced her first shattering street encounter.

It was seven o'clock on a Monday morning, and Ruby was on her way to her job at the coffee shop. As always, numerous addicts and homeless lined the steps, landings and lobby of her building.

As she reached the fourth floor, she had to sidestep a sleeping derelict sprawled on the landing. His hand abruptly shot out, grabbed her ankle and threw her off balance. Ruby fell hard onto the cracked tile floor, hitting her forehead on the step. Her uniform was askew, exposing her white cotton panties and stocking covered thighs. Ruby quickly pulled her dress down to cover herself.

"Where you rushin' off to, sweet thing? Why don't you jus' sit here and keep me company for awhile?" The words dribbled out of the man's crust- cornered mouth as his beady eyes focused on Ruby's shaking hands. She was clamping her waitress uniform firmly over her thighs.

Still firmly holding her ankle, the man smirked

maliciously. "What you hidin' under there, Missy?" His eyes were fixed on Ruby's trembling thighs and tense hands.

Ruby tried to inch away from him, but the more she moved, the more intense his grasp became. Her whisper was pitiful. "Mister, I have to go work. I'll lose my job." In response to her plea, the man emitted an evil chuckle, then cynically laughed out loud.

The trespasser looked at Ruby's face for the first time. The utter fear in her eyes excited him. Then he noticed the large red scar embedded in her cheek. The gyrating keloid ominously stared back at him.

"What the hell is that on your face? It sure is ugly."

For a fleeting moment, Ruby thought he would let her go. Perhaps her blemish would save her, like Ruth in the Bible. In that moment, he forcefully flipped her to a prone position, causing her again to hit her head on the step. He pulled her dress above her hips and ruthlessly yanked her panties down to expose her buttocks. Ruby's desperate cry echoed through the landings of the tenement. It was a wail that went unanswered.

The molester pulled out a knife and held it to Ruby's throat. His foul, heaving breath rested heavily on the back of her neck. "You do that again and I'll give you a matching scar for the other cheek."

Ruby remained silent as the invader continued his assault. Hot tears soaked her face, blurring her vision and adding to the wooziness she felt after hitting her head on the step.

One of Ma 'Dear's sayings eased its way into her consciousness. "You ain't lucky nor 'specially blessed, Baby." It rang true.

Ruby found herself focusing on the grey and black hairs standing erect on the man's ashy arms. His too long nails were encrusted with black debris. She began to count his violent thrusts. It reminded her of the sexual encounters she had had with her husband. In that moment, she was glad she had killed Harold.

By the time, she counted twelve thrusts, Ruby's mind went blank. She felt numb. Her attacker finally fell into an intoxicated sleep. Ruby was able to free herself from his weight. Back on her feet, she felt wobbly and nauseous.

Her olfactory lobe was assaulted with the overwhelming odor of alcohol, feces, urine, sweat and semen. She vomited multiple times until nothing was left except the bitter taste of bile in her mouth.

After a failed attempt to smooth out her disheveled uniform, she stumbled down the four remaining flights of stairs, out of the building and onto the streets of Harlem, unsure of her next step. Silently, she vowed never to return to her room in the tenement, not even to get her few belongings.

She walked aimlessly in the direction of St. Thomas the Apostle Church on 119th Street, passing two policemen. The officers did not seem to notice her. Ruby wanted to run to them and scream out her story. She could not bring herself to repeat what had just happened to her. She was just in too much pain and was so embarrassed.

Next to the church was a shelter that was always full by mid-morning. Ruby staggered in. An attendant, noting her condition, led her to a cot, no questions asked. She fell promptly into a deep sleep.

When she awoke, it was late morning. The events of the previous day were a blur, almost surreal. Ruby wondered if the assault had occurred or if it had just been a horrific nightmare. The burning, raw pain between her legs and the aching and shooting pain in her anal area would not permit a disavowal. Then she looked down at her stained uniform and torn stockings. Reality overcame her as soft moans escaped from her bruised mouth.

In the shelter's bathroom, Ruby stared at her reflection in the mirror and started to cry. It was a low cry, muffled, so that other residents could not hear her. She had a lemon-sized black and blue knot on her forehead, her eyes were red and swollen to squints. There were multiple abrasions on her face and dried tear stains mixed with crusted mucous around her nose. The smells of the assailant still lingered on her person and clothes.

Picking up the bar of brown soap sitting on the sink, she ran the hot water and used paper towels to clean off the remains of the attack. Gingerly, she removed her stockings, careful not to further aggravate her bruised knees. The dried caked blood was stuck to her knees and stockings pulling at the contusion which throbbed beneath it. She discarded the nylons in the trash receptacle. Next, she removed her panties, and saw a revolting, stained mess of blood, urine and semen. Using the soap, she vigorously scrubbed the soiled underwear. Her efforts at removing the stains from her uniform were unsuccessful.

Ruby gave herself a paper towel shower, delicately cleaning her burning and sore private areas. She put the cleaned, still wet underwear back on. Its dampness offered some cooling relief to the injured area.

She had a sixteen-block walk to her job at the deli. Since it was already hot outside, Ruby figured she would be almost dry by the time she reached work. When she walked into the deli, her boss took one look at her. "You're fired," he said. "You missed yesterday and come in today like something the cat dragged in."

He asked no questions and Ruby offered no explanation. Embarrassed by the stares of the customers who were having their morning coffee and bagels, she turned around and headed back to the shelter. The volunteers there gave her a white tee shirt and a pair of baggy khakis. This would be her new uniform for the next 20 years. Unable to find employment over the following months, Ruby went from the shelter to the streets.

Her gaze turned back to the mysterious iris duo staring back expectantly into her own hazel colored pair. Ruby wondered how long it had taken her to mentally recall the details of her violent event of 20 years ago.

Raising her left hand, which was still holding the

eggplant skin, Ruby offered the dark purple peel to the seated man. Her voice was a whisper, barely audible above the traffic sounds of 125th Street and Amsterdam.

"This is your skin-mate, Eggplant Man." Ruby had audaciously renamed the stranger.

CHAPTER 4

Eggplant Man

Intrigued, Eggplant Man looked at the piece of glistening purple skin in Ruby's hand. He took mental note of her caramel fingers and the gentle way she was caressing the vegetable peel. There was no doubt in his mind that he would accept this unusual gift. He could not recall the last time anyone had given him anything, other than the suit he was wearing.

He had never eaten the vegetable but recognized it and its resemblance to his own coloring. Always sensitive to his dark skin, he thought for a moment that Ruby might have been trying to insult him. One glance into her eyes assured him that was not the case.

His mind traveled back to earlier days growing up in the mulatto section of New Orleans, where skin color was a dividing factor within the social, political and religious echelons and even within family structures. It often was a determining feature in the course your life would take, whom you would marry, where you would live and what clubs you would frequent.

*"There was a time when I would shrink and want
to fade
away
When I was told, I looked like ink by some ignorant
ofay
Faithfully I'd fry my naps so that no one could see
That my hair in its natural state was kinky as could be"*

His pigment had made him a frequent object of jokes and prejudice within his own race. To the white world, he was considered more of a threat than his lighter-skinned brothers who, due to their Creole mix, often appeared white. Had he finally overcome the ridicule?

"Now I walk with head held high
And wisdom under my cap
Knowing that my fear did die
And it's beautiful to be black"

Eggplant Man finally reached out, accepting the remarkable skin-matched item from Ruby. He was careful to touch her hand in the process...and she noticed. He was amazed at the eggplant's smoothness and texture. He thought that God surely must have had this vegetable in mind when he created his skin tone.

He also liked the new name given to him by this scarred, gentle lady. It suited him much better than his family given name of LeRoy Vaughn Reed, which meant small, red-haired king.

Eggplant Man looked at Ruby with a sudden intensity, eye to eye, hand to hand. "Thank you, Ruby," he said in a voice so deep and reverberating that it startled Ruby. The hustle bustle of the people surrounding her, heading to and from their lunch hour, halted for a second. They stared. The three words were the first he had uttered to another person in six years. Eggplant Man had not engaged in any conversations since his friend Joe, Bubba's son and the original owner of the barber shop, went back to Mississippi. One green-black skinned lady, in a bright yellow dress and matching yellow shoes, sauntered over to where the two new 'friends' were sitting. She dropped a dollar into the cup, which Eggplant Man always kept near his large crusted feet. Ruby shot a darting, unfriendly glance at the woman.

Eggplant Man looked at the woman in yellow. She could have been his sister. She had very dark, smooth skin and an afro hairdo of coarse salt and pepper tight coils. Observing her bright dress, he recalled admonitions to dark-complexioned Blacks in the South regarding dress codes. Eggplant Man could not help creating a silent bluesy refrain.

"Hey black gal in that yellow dress
As fine as fine can be
Didn't your mama always stress
That color's not for thee
Nor is orange, red, lime or white
For it emphasizes your constant plight
And brings attention for all to see
That black, black color that you be"

Ruby abruptly stood up and turned away, heading back to her garbage expedition. She now had only one hour left before the trash would be picked up and the treasures therein forever lost.

Eggplant Man returned to his reclining position. Watching Ruby's disjointed movements on her way back to her obsessive search, he fingered the purple skin one more time before he gingerly slid it into the left jacket pocket right over his heart.

CHAPTER 5

A Good Omen

Ruby's mind was racing as she returned to the garbage cans. Only twelve more cans to go.

She could not release the recent encounter with the Eggplant Man from her mind. "He touched my scar," she thought. "Nobody ever touches me...nobody!" And no one had touched Ruby in 20 years. "Did I hear him say Ruby?" His deep voice was echoing in her head. "Ruby, Ruby, Ruby!"

Her scar was still tingling from the abrasive yet gentle stroke of his rough fingertip. Ruby felt a little dizzy...too many thoughts running in her head, like a piglet on the loose. "How did he know my name?" she asked herself.

As she reached 127th and Amsterdam, Ruby methodically surveyed the overflowing garbage cans, lined up and impatiently awaiting the disposal trucks' routine arrival. It became a game for her. Could she finish her garbage tour before the trucks arrived? If she completed her task before the trucks came into view, she believed something serendipitous would happen the next week. The previous week, she had beaten the trucks by 15 minutes… and this week there was Eggplant Man.

Diligently, she began rummaging through can one, finding nothing of interest. The garbage receptacles were filled with rotting, half-eaten burgers, candy wrappers, sticky cans, and both new and crumpled newspapers, soiled baby diapers, soda bottles, one still with a swig left in the bottom . "Why didn't they finish it all?" she thought, as she swallowed the remaining liquid in the soda bottle.

Ruby was always intrigued by newspapers. She read only the headlines. The whole story was of little significance to her. Her mind recalled the **Metairie Daily** headlines of December 25, 20 years earlier: ***"Woman Kills Husband After Having Face Slashed."*** The caption was accompanied by an enlarged, hypnotic picture of Ruby. The still raw C-shaped scar dominated her left cheek.

"Nobody cared about the whole story," she thought. "Only the condemning headlines were important to them."

Can two, three, four… more of the same. Ah, at last she arrived at can 12, and no truck in sight. As she was searching the last can, she noticed mahogany colored roaches scattering about and began to count them. There were 12. Twelve roaches in can 12…another good omen for the next week. She never harmed the roaches. They were survivors just like her.

Ruby was now carrying ten crumpled and some hardly

read newspapers, evenly distributed under each arm. She never took more than she could easily carry. Her mother's voice rang in her ears: "Never take on more than you can handle, Baby."

Ruby's reply to any request made by her mother was always the same, "Yes, Ma'Dear." Her mother called her 'Baby' right up to age 17. That year, Ma'Dear and Ruby's only sibling, Jon-Jon, were killed in a house fire. Her mother had returned home, exhausted after cleaning Missy Mays' two story house all day. While preparing dinner for Jon-Jon and Ruby, she left the food cooking on the stove and fell asleep on the living room couch. A fire broke out. Her two-year-old brother was trapped in his room. Ruby was at school helping to decorate the gym for prom night. The headlines read: ***"Mother and Son Burned to Death in Fire."*** The rest of the story was unimportant. It never even mentioned how tired her mother was.

Ruby was heading back to her 'space' when she noticed out of the corner of her nystagmus glance the grey garbage truck turning onto 127th Street. She had beaten it again!

"Next week will be a good one," she thought.

CHAPTER 6

Playing the Blues is Like....

Eggplant Man had watched Ruby as she abruptly rose and walked away...leaving her scent still lingering in his air. Her slight form was engulfed by her rumpled baggy khakis. Her shiny black braids, jumping up and down on her shoulders, kept rhythm with her staccato steps. The innate musician in him created jazz to match the braid-beat.

"Exotic sounds of distant drums, ride
On cool breezes, in synchrony (plopity-plop)
With the ebb and flow
Of warm wet indigo waves (plopity-plop)
Keeping perfect rhythm
With the beat of the congas (plopity- plop)"

He reached into his pocket and felt the smooth surface of the vegetable skin resting there. It was warm now, lying over his heart. His right index finger was still transmitting messages to his brain about the soft feeling of Ruby's keloid scar against his calloused finger.

Eggplant Man was startled suddenly by a stranger's intrusion. A tall, distinguished looking figure in a cream-colored linen suit, a tan Stetson hat and brown and white Spectator shoes, was standing in front of his open banjo case. The man was holding what looked like a neatly folded bill in his hand. Eggplant Man could see only the corner of the money, but he thought it might be a ten spot. He straightened up slightly. "That could be lunch and dinner for me and … for me." He mused at his Ruby inclusive thought.

The gentleman had a demeanor of both expectancy and patience reflected in his face. He seemed to sense that the banjo player was deep in thought and respectfully declined to interrupt him.

Eggplant Man felt the stranger was about to say something to him, but he kept his face expressionless, his eyes straight ahead, saying nothing. He just waited, giving him non-verbal permission to proceed. He thought, "Just drop the money in the banjo case, Mister, and go on with your life."

"I bet you don't know 'Damn Right I Got the Blues'," the stranger said finally.

Just hearing the name of the Buddy Guy piece struck a

chord deep in Eggplant Man's soul, from a time that seemed so long ago.

Buddy Guy was a Louisiana 'boy,' just like him. He played his guitar and beat it with drumsticks at the same time. He had heard Guy play in Baton Rouge and had had the honor of sharing the stage with him at the NO Jazz Club when the famed musician passed through Metairie in 1974. As a young teen, Eggplant Man used to hang out at jazz joints waiting to hear the jazz greats as they passed through his town. One of the great highlights of his life was playing at the 10th Annual New Orleans Jazz Festival in 1978. He got to jam with greats like Eubie Blake, James Booker, Charlie Mingus and Roosevelt Sykes (***The Honey Dripper***).

Frequently, these jazz greats would let him sit in on a set and play his guitar or banjo on stage with them. His idol was Buddy Guy, but he never got to Guy's performances in Chicago as he had promised himself. Serving that jail time had gotten in the way.

Buddy Guy was a legend. Asking him if he knew Buddy's work was like asking him if he remembered how Ruby smelled… like cinnamon, coconut and ripe honeydew floating in summer sweat.

"Sweet Jesus!" he said aloud.

His hand instinctively felt for the tautness of his banjo strings, directing his mind away from other strained areas. The obedient banjo threads robotically surrendered to their master and, unprompted, the melody flowed. The words began to tumble out of his mouth in a smooth Louisiana drawl.

You damn right, I've got the blues,
From my head, down to my shoes
You damn right, I've got the blues,
From my head down to my shoes
I can't win, cause I don't have a thing to lose...

His fingers continued plucking at the guitar strings even after the words ended. The stranger's head and feet were tapping to the beat, joining him in a sort of exotic trance created by the music. When Eggplant Man finished the last note of his 'bluesy' serenade, the man dropped the bill into the banjo case. It was a twenty. As he walked off, still bopping his head, the stranger muttered, "That was all right man, it was all right."

Eggplant Man picked up the crisp bill, unfolded and refolded it, and stuck it in the top part of his torn sock. He decided it was enough for the day, closed his banjo case and headed east on 127th Street. It had been a good day.

He passed a tall brown-skinned lady dressed in different shades of blue. He had noticed her listening to his Buddy Guy rendition. She said nothing, and dropped nothing into his banjo case. He could feel her eyes on him as he walked by, but he made no effort to return her stare.

CHAPTER 7

Primal Loss

It was just past four in the afternoon and it was still hot and muggy in August Harlem. It reminded Ruby of summer in Louisiana, but the smells and sounds were so different. She had always been one who paid attention to smells. Odors brought back vivid and detailed memories, as if the event connected to that smell was occurring in that very moment. As a child, everything she picked up she brought first to her nose: pencils, blocks, dolls, food, paper clips…it didn't matter. Her nose was like a clearing house before any further action could take place. Ma'Dear would always say, "Baby, you knows you gets a piece of everythin' you smell, inside you." Ruby replied, "Yes, Ma'Dear." Keeping that in mind, Ruby practiced holding her breath at the first hint of an odor that repulsed her. The odor of burnt anything was particularly difficult for her, bringing back the day of her high school prom.

Ruby had rushed home to tell Ma'Dear that she had

finished decorating the dance hall. She decided she was going to wear her hair up after all. More importantly, Jerome, her date and the object of her fantasized romance, had winked at her and said, "See you later, Ruby." Her already weak knees gave way when she arrived home. Her house was burnt to the ground, a pile of steaming ash, with only two blackened appliances, the stove and refrigerator, still standing upright, as if in defiance to the fates. Her mother and brother were somewhere in the smoking rubble.

The smell was overwhelming. It was a haunting combination of burnt rubber, wood, fabric, food, flesh and burnt hair. The smell of the hair was the thing that remained indelible, almost alive in her brain. Ruby remembered inhaling deeply. She wanted it to become a part of her.

CHAPTER 8

The Abode

There were still a few more hours of daylight. She was heading downtown to 119th Street. Getting settled in for the night early was routine for Ruby. There was a block between Amsterdam and Broadway that had several abandoned buildings. Even these well boarded-up structures were unable to escape infiltration by those who had nowhere else to go. The poor, the homeless, those floating in nebulous clouds of addiction and those maneuvering through the mental world of dysfunctions and disconnection mingled together in this implausible community. All of them were trying to hold onto or escape their individual nightmare paradigms.

Ruby stayed in the last building on the block. Several years before, she had managed to pry open a metal sheet from a window in the back alley of the apartment building. Since you had to have an address to qualify for state financial assistance, Ruby had for the past 12 years used this address at the welfare office to receive her Medicaid checks. She would wait for the mailman out front, on the first and the 15th of each month. For his own safety, the postman would arrive in the early morning, before the addicts and hoodlums arose. Ruby had an unspoken agreement with him. He delivered her illicit remunerations each month. Although he was aware of Ruby's homelessness, his compassion overruled him. He continued the delivery over the years. Each time he would warn Ruby of the dangers of street living. This is how she survived. Ruby cashed her paltry checks at the liquor store on the corner of 125th and Amsterdam.

The back-alley window was the entrance to a sub-ground level space that had probably been used as an office/apartment for the former apartment manager. Ruby sometimes would imagine that she was the manager of the building and this was her office. Her small frame slid easily under the metal sheet and her feet landed on top of an old splintered wood desk, directly under the window. The metal sheet closed shut behind her.

It was dark in there, with only a sliver of light shining over the top of another window boarded with wood from the inside. This window was the only other one in the apartment. Ruby had a collection of candles of all sizes, shapes and aromas. She lit three this afternoon. A lot was on her mind. She did not light any of the scented candles. The aromas would distract her and she wanted to vividly recall the events of the day.

Inside the space was a cot with several old blankets neatly

folded on top, a broken wood swivel chair, a refrigerator and small stove, neither of which worked due to lack of electricity in the building. There was a small dilapidated bathroom whose rusty shower faucet continuously trickled a thin stream of cold water. It had broken tiled floors and walls, and a sometimes-flushing toilet, with the help of added water to both the bowl and the tank behind it. The sink did not work at all. Ruby kept bottles of water which she collected from a faucet in the alley behind Wong's Chinese Take-out, two blocks away.

She also had a huge collection of newspapers stored in the non-working kitchen. These served a double purpose. Paper proved to be great for keeping warm. On exceptionally cold nights, Ruby would pile a combination of five Daily News and five Amsterdam News papers on top of her, two blankets underneath her, and then two blankets on top of the newspapers. This worked. She also read the headlines on all of the newspapers… only the headlines. Ma'Dear would say, "The whole story is in the headlines, Baby."

Ruby sat on the cot and brought her left hand to her nose. This caused her fingers to tremble slightly. The lingering scent of the eggplant skin rested there. She recalled the color and texture of the skin gleaming in the hot Harlem sun. The taste of her mother's special eggplant, peppers, and tomato dish flooded her mouth, which had already begun to water.

Another scent impatiently waited to burst forth. She knew what it was. It refused to be ignored. Her index finger instinctively touched her left cheek and traced the path the calloused finger had coursed earlier that day. Her hand then returned faithfully to her nose, obeying some unspoken order. The smell of cloves, tobacco and Belgium chocolate mingled with summer sweat aroused Ruby's olfactory. The manliness of this mélange of scents was captivating.

It had been a long time since Ruby had allowed her thoughts to venture into that realm. All of this thinking, combined with the day's events, was unsettling and made her tired. A sensation was growing inside her chest, warm and thick like syrup and slowly drizzling over her heart. "Painless," she thought.

Ruby did not want to worry about this new, pleasurable feeling. She felt a little dizzy, perhaps giddy, and could feel the sandman closing her eyes. Her fatigue overcame her. There had been too much thinking today.

Ruby removed her khakis and tee shirt, folded them and placed them into her faux dresser, made from two cardboard boxes. She kept her bra on this evening, in an effort to contain that tingly sensation in her chest. It had now spread to her breasts. She did remove her panties. Noticing a whitish discharge in the crotch, she methodically washed them in the one stream of cold water that continuously flowed from the shower. She used a harsh brown bar soap.

On Friday nights, and on some Saturday mornings, St. Thomas the Apostle Church--on 118th Street just west of St. Nicholas Avenue--distributed to the homeless items like soap, shampoo, toilet paper, candles and other miscellaneous items. Ruby treasured her coarse soap. She used it to clean everything, including her face and body. Today, though, she was careful not to wash her scar. Instead, she ran her right index finger over the length of her lesion.

She managed to extinguish the candles one by one with her right thumb and index finger, allowing the smell of Eggplant Man to be sealed there by the warm wax. She slid into her makeshift bed, covered up with the newspaper of the day, and let her eyelids softly meet. Her right hand remained at smelling distance from her nose. For the first time in 20 years, Ruby had forgotten to read the headlines before going to sleep.

CHAPTER 9
No Escape

mary wont ya come out of yonder tree mary cuz i want you down here with me see i know the place with the good fried chicken with biscuits and gravy and all the mixin's hey mary, don choo wanna? mary wont you come wit me? mary don ya hide under all them books sweet little girl with them bad good looks see i know the place ...

From *Lyrics* Mania

Eggplant Man could not get Ruby out of his head. The intensity of her brief yet compelling, hazel-eyed stare remained with him, flashing back sporadically throughout the day.

His gastric juices began to flow. Now, he felt hungry. Knowing that he had missed lunch at the soup kitchen on 125th and St. Nicholas, he reversed his direction and began heading west on 127th, telling himself he would go to the Down-home stand on 125th street that boasted 'Southern-Style' fast food. Subtly looking north and south on each block, he pretended he wasn't searching, but secretly hoped to see Ruby walking there. He gazed down at his sock and saw the slight bulge of the 20-dollar bill he had placed there. It was enough to buy two meals for two people. "Dinner and breakfast," he thought. He smiled to himself at the absurdity of his fantasy. Ruby was nowhere in sight. Little did Eggplant Man know, Ruby was busy elsewhere, having her own thoughts.

Not fully acknowledging his disappointment, he arrived at the food-stand, ordered two pieces of fried chicken and a biscuit with gravy. Instead of talking, he pointed to the items on the menu taped to the counter. The total cost for all was one dollar and seventy-five cents. None of it tasted like 'down-home' anything. Hungry, he wolfed down the impostors.

Already disappointed at not seeing Ruby, he eyed the two cooks in the kitchen suspiciously. One was Asian and the other Latino. Eggplant Man sent the pair a non-verbal message: "Are you kidding me with this food?" They avoided his gaze, both guiltily looking downward at the bubbling old cooking oil.

"Ain't nothing like the chicken at Willie Mae's Scotch House on St. Ann's Street in New Orleans," he thought.

Willie Mae had the best fried chicken he had ever tasted. She was in that kitchen frying it up all by herself. Ms. Mae used a secret ingredient she wouldn't share with anyone. "It's just love, baby," she would say. People would come from hundreds of miles away just to taste that love.

It was starting to cool off a bit, so Eggplant Man considered his sleeping plans for the evening. The mission would already be full by this time, so it would have to be a night in the park or in a doorway. Mr. Lee, owner of Bubba's Barber shop, did not like it when he spent the night in front of the barber shop. Most of the barbers that worked at the shop were black. There was one Puerto Rican guy, but the owner was Mr. Lee.

In a thick Chinese accent, Mr. Lee would shout, "Not good for business! You can't sleep here!"

But Eggplant Man wanted to stay there and reminisce about the day's events. He wondered where Ruby was and what she was thinking.

The shop used to be owned by Old Joe, from Mississippi. Joe had cut hair for most of his life, since he was 10. His father, Joe Brown, Sr., had owned a shop in Tupelo, Mississippi, right across from Oxford, where Elvis Presley was born. Joe would say that his Daddy cut the hair of most of the black boys in Tupelo, and many of the white boys too, who grew up in Tupelo. He was the best barber in town. They called him Poppa Joe.

With the civil rights movement of the 60's, things got very tense in Tupelo and Poppa Joe was forced to close his shop. He had slipped and made a racial comment in front of a little white boy whose hair he was cutting. After closing his shop, Poppa Joe fell into a state of depression and suffered a heart attack, dying soon afterwards.

Joe, whom everyone called Bubba, then came north to seek work as a barber and had been there in Harlem for years. He would give Eggplant Man odd jobs around the shop and let him sleep there whenever he wanted.

From time to time, Bubba managed to convince him to let him cut off an inch or two of his hair. Eggplant Man liked having his hair at least four inches long in an "afro" crown style. When he was in prison, it was mandatory to keep his hair very short. The prison barber had made it a point to nick his scalp each time he cut his hair. Once free, Bubba decided to let his hair grow.

When Bubba wasn't cutting hair, he and Eggplant Man, known to him as LeRoy, would talk for hours about Jazz, the Blues and women. Both were big fans of Ella Fitzgerald, Bessie Smith, Lady Day and Louis Armstrong. At the end of a good day, Eggplant Man would play "St. Louis Blues" on his banjo and Bubba would sing the lyrics.

I hate to see that evening sun go down
I hate to see that evening sun go down
Cause my lovin' baby done left this town

If I feel tomorrow like I feel today
If I feel tomorrow like I feel today
I'm gonna pack my trunk and make my
getaway

A Ruby thought flashed across his mind. "What if she don't come back?" he thought. He felt a slight tightening in his throat and then quickly returned his thoughts to Bubba.

Six years ago, when Bubba's mother fell ill, he decided to go back home to Tupelo, to take care of her. When she died, he sold his shop in Harlem and stayed in Mississippi to reconnect with his family. He had always talked about going back home.

Eventually, he did. Eggplant Man missed his only friend and had not spoken with anyone for the six years since his buddy had left.

He decided to sleep on top of some wood planks in the alley behind the shop. Piled about four feet high, the wood was left over from the renovation of a clothes shop located a few doors down from the barber shop. He removed his jacket and rolled it up, forming a crude pillow, then climbed easily onto the makeshift lumber bed. He laid on his good side, rested his head on his jacket, checked his sock for his money, and closed his eyes. His hand sought his groin as he allowed his thoughts to drift to Ruby.

CHAPTER 10

Lured

Ruby tossed and turned for most of the night. A song Ma'Dear often used to sing kept playing in her head.

A good man is hard to find, you always get
the other kind
Just when you think that he's your pal
You look for him and find him foolin'
around some other gal
— en you rave, you even crave to see him
layin in his grave
So if you man is nice, take my advice...

A Good Man is Hard to Find, Alberta Hunter- lyrics, Lovie Austin- composer

When she awoke the next morning, Ruby did not feel rested and was annoyed with herself for waking up so late. It was already 9:30 AM, which meant she had missed the 7 AM garbage rounds. She moved quickly toward the bathroom, almost stepping on a mouse darting across the floor in the opposite direction. Ruby never attempted to interrupt or harm any creature she categorized as a survivor. There seemed to be a mutual respect between them and her. Flies were the only exception. No qualms about putting an early end to their twenty-one day lives.

Ruby rinsed the night from her face, slipped on her now dry panties, her torn baggy khakis and a white tee from her collection of them, all from the mission. She kept the tee shirts on top of the rickety desk, neatly folded in a stack, in one of the cardboard boxes that served as her makeshift dresser. All of the shirts were white and plain, without any message or writing on them. She did not want to give people reason to look at her. Ruby unplaited her rope thick, shoulder length braids, ritually applied coconut oil to both her hair and scalp, brushed her hair 113 strokes and re-plaited her braids into two symmetrical, gleaming rows.

Ma' Dear's voice echoed in her head. "A woman's hair is her crown an' glory, baby, you gotta' make it pretty every day…100 brushes and coconut oil. Men loves a woman with pretty hair." "Yes, Ma'Dear," Ruby said aloud in the moment. Today, Ruby wanted her hair to be extra pretty. She added 13 extra strokes, since it was the 13th of August.

She took one of her shower stream refilled bottles of

water, climbed onto the desk, slipped through the metal flap covering the window-space and headed out, acting as if she had no plans.

Her not so hidden agenda was to mosey on over to 125th Street. She wanted to catch a casual glimpse of Eggplant Man in front of Bubba's.

This thought had not fully reached her consciousness, but the warm syrup feeling began to rise again in her chest. It had begun to drizzle downward to her abdomen.

Ruby was thirsty this morning and quickly finished the water she was carrying. She never littered the street. Dutifully, she dropped her empty water bottle in a nearby empty trash can, remembering her mother's words:

"Baby, ain't no maids here, put it where it's 'sposed to go."

"Yes, Ma 'Dear."

It was now 10 blocks to her destination and Ruby felt as if she were moving in slow motion. People seemed to be constantly in her way, annoying her. Her choppy walking style sometimes caused people momentarily to stop in their tracks, hesitating about which way to go. Ruby hated those dancing encounters, a brief forced intimate moment with a stranger, interrupting her flow. As she finally rounded the corner of 125th and Amsterdam, her heart momentarily stopped, skipping a beat and causing a swirl in her head. There he was, back erect, as if he were again holding up the wall to the parlor.

At 10 in the morning, the sun was already hot. Its rays, streaming down, seemed to spotlight him, his four inch "crown" and his smooth dark-purple glowing skin. As he strummed on his banjo with those long calloused fingers, Ruby thought about the rough fingertip that had coursed the length of her scar the day before. The sticky river descended further down her abdomen. She could barely breathe. Was she still walking or standing still? She did not know.

CHAPTER 11

Something's coming, something good

Eggplant Man had risen early that morning: about 6:30 AM. He had slept surprisingly well. He knew Ruby was usually out early making her garbage can rounds. Not wanting to miss her, he quickly rinsed his face with water from an alley faucet and performed his sparse version of a wash-up. He had a routine of morning cat stretches that helped eliminate his lower back pain. The discomfort was a consequence of too many years of sleeping on cement, in doorways and on cots at the mission.

Adjusting the strings on his banjo, he checked his sock for his $18 and 25 cents, and headed for his spot in front of Bubba's. He arrived there so quickly he could not even recall the six-block walk. Casually, Eggplant Man began surveying the people traffic on Amsterdam Avenue. There were very few pedestrians on the street that morning. He could tell already, it was going to be another hot and humid August day.

For months, he had seen Ruby from a distance, a female entity, routinely searching and collecting garbage three times each week. Eggplant Man did not pay much attention to her. She was just a part of the city's daily humdrum. However, yesterday was a completely different story. It had been up close, personal and spellbinding. As soon as he'd seen her face, those hypnotic eyes and the indelible C-shaped scar, he'd remembered her story and her name as if it had just happened.

He recalled how he'd felt when he read the story in the Metairie news and saw her pitiful face staring back from the front page. He knew she would be ostracized, as only a small town could do. She was young, not 18 years old, and had no close relatives except her father, who had abandoned the family years before this incident. Her father returned home after hearing of the death of his wife and son. He did not know what to do with his 17-year-old. She had been staying with disgruntled relatives. So, he married the teenager off, to Harold, a man twice her age. The hope was that Harold would take care of Ruby, ending his own responsibility as her father.

Ruby's husband turned out to be an abusive alcoholic, like her own father. Several months after the tragic murder event occurred, gossip had it that Ruby had moved north to stay with a distant aunt. Her father had died two years after her marriage to Harold.

Ruby was now on her own. The trial was quick and the

verdict, mercifully, was self-defense. But the town was not empathetic and vicious whispers followed Ruby wherever she went, even to church. Church was normally the one place people in the South could always go for solace and support. Eggplant Man wondered, at that time, what a young girl in her position would do.

CHAPTER 12
The Gift of Music

Eggplant Man knew the South and its rules very well. He was born in New Orleans, Lower Ninth Ward. His family was very poor. In September 1955, A horrific hurricane struck New Orleans with a vengeance. The storm took a total of eighty-one lives. Eighty percent of the Lower Ninth Ward district was under water, including his already dilapidated abode. Following the storm, people walked through water that for some was above their waists, holding children in their arms, to escape the flood. Eggplant Man was one of those children. Shortly after saving his son's life, the boy's father fell ill and died from pneumonia.

Eggplant Man's family moved to Mississippi to live with relatives for five years. His mother remarried and returned to Metairie, where he lived until he was seventeen.

What he remembered most about his father was his love of music. A lot happened in the South, in the mid-1900s, to any Black man trying to survive. No matter what transpired, his father played his 'gitar' every day.

"Boy, music can save yo' life. The power is in them strings." Then he would laugh, a deep dark reverberating guffaw, and tell the story of Samson and Delilah.

"Don't never let nobody clip yo' strings. You hear me, boy?"

"Yes, sir," replied Lil' Roy, as he was called at that time.

Eggplant Man started playing his father's guitar when he was two years old. His father was called Big Roy. He had taught his son how to play. The guitar came naturally to L'il Roy. People said "he had the gift." It always seemed to calm him down. Besides music, L'il Roy had no other passion. His temperament was pensive, quiet and a bit melancholic…a born observer. His mother was like that. Her advice to him, on more than one occasion: "Don't speak 'less ya' spoken to, boy, don't ya' say nothin' 'less it make a difference o' save yo' life. Amen, son?" His mother always punctuated her sentences with 'Amen or God-willin'. "Amen, Ma'am," was his usual reply of accord.

CHAPTER 13

Love is a Strange Thing

Eggplant Man could recall feeling this way only once before, some 30 years ago, before his incarceration. He was sitting at the bar, between sets at the famous Tricou House Jazz Club on Bourbon Street, New Orleans.

It was the summer of 1970. The Tricou Club was smoky and humid, its legendary blue light casting a soft hazy aura around everyone there. Legend also has it, this Jazz Club was haunted as well, by the Tricou family, the eccentric original owners of the house. In the midst of the haze, he found himself entranced by a curvaceous, sultry "mucho choco-latte" high-heeled lady in a fitted red dress.

Eggplant Man very easily recalled that scarlet garb. It was clinging for life to every curve God had so graciously given the woman. Instead of walking, she sauntered into the club. That lady was swaying those talking hips and bouncing her bouncy butt at the same time. It was art in motion. The beginning of a lifetime haunting memory had begun.

The Cheshire grin plastered on his face must have been what led her straight over to his bar stool. Enticed, she asked him to dance. It was one of those slow and easy, up close and personal, bluesy grinds. By the time the dance was over he was lost in her perfume, his sweat, the blue haze, the red dress. He missed his next set and spent the next three nights wrapped in her chocolate and her black satin sheets. He cried out for Mercy! God granted him none. They remained lovers and became great friends.

For six months, it was an easy flowing, sexy relationship, with lots of laughter and good times. Then one day it ended, just as it had started. She put on her red dress and high-heels and sauntered her 'jiggly' butt and all that came with it right out the front door. There was no goodbye, no explanation. Her name was Lula Belle Devereaux.

He had a tight icy hot squeeze in his chest for months. That affair was the last time he truly awakened the dragon. After that affair, staying above his emotions became his 'modus operandi.'

After the Lula Belle situation, Eggplant Man decided to head north. He wanted a new start in the big city. He moved around like a nomad all through the south, playing gigs in many jazz clubs and meeting many of the jazz and blues greats. On his route to the Big Apple, Eggplant Man stopped in Selma, and got involved in a brawl that had broken out in a small juke joint. This led to a 15 year detour in a Selma prison, serving hard labor, for a crime he never committed. He and his banjo finally arrived in 1985, in

New York City. Despite every-thing that had transpired, he still held hope for a new life.

Eggplant Man turned his thoughts back into the present moment. He looked at the money bulge in his sock, felt for the vegetable skin still in his jacket pocket and resumed strumming the banjo strings.

Lay on my soil and enjoy its richness
Let your roots absorb my moisture
Dancing on thoughts of yesterday's dreams
Free to roam the world touching even the
unsuspecting

Eggplant Man tried to recall other times he had had any deep sentiments for a woman. He remembered Faye, his wife of one year. She had just turned 18 and he was 19. They had spent his junior and senior years of high school together, infatuated with each other. It was puppy love for sure. They knew very little of what it would take to make a marriage work; both were too young and immature. But they got married one week after graduation.

After high school, Eggplant Man was always on the road, moving from gig to gig. Faye stayed home; young, beautiful, bored and lonely. She eventually ran off with a local and remarried.

Then, of course, there was Lula Belle Devereaux. There was no forgetting that one. Eggplant Man could not recall the details of his other short lived relationships, a blur of meaningless encounters. Now there was Ruby.

Eggplant Man decided to get some coffee and biscuits. Feeling totally unprepared and betrayed by his heart, he needed time to think. He thought about how this Ruby encounter was so unexpected.

CHAPTER 14
Every Man Needs a Song

Eggplant Man returned his thoughts to Ruby. According to the clock on the wall in Bubba's parlor, it was now 8:30 A.M. and there was no sign of her anywhere. Perhaps she was not coming back after yesterday. That thought, created a slight tightening in his throat, which he cleared in an effort to gain some control over the feeling. He started to strum his banjo as a calming device. Just the memory of the previous day's events reawakened the smell of coconut in his nostrils.

He tried to avoid looking up the street. He tried to convince himself that he was not anxious. At 9:55, after what seemed like a year's penance in purgatory, he looked towards Amsterdam and there she stood, not moving. Was she staring at him? He continued to strum his banjo, looking at her, feeling the droplets of sweat accumulate on his brow, his upper lip and in his armpits. He saw her turn abruptly and head in the other direction. His heart began to pound, beating against the eggplant skin in his left upper inside jacket pocket. The skin began to feel weighted against his chest. Had he scared her, by using her name? "Thank you, Ruby," he had said. He had wanted to explain, but after six years of silence, his words had come slowly, and she'd left so quickly. He sank into thought for a few minutes.

When he looked up, an attractive brown-skinned lady stood there in her house dress. Her eyes were red and puffy and there were tear stains on her cheeks. Her lower lip was cut and dried blood caked both corners of her mouth. Her hardened expression told him that this woman had been around the block more than a few times. The woman was probably in her mid-thirties, but looked a lot older. Life had been difficult for her. There were signs of ongoing abuse, but she wasn't leaving her abuser. It was too painful to look her in the eye, so Eggplant Man looked away.

"Sing this Mississippi River brown gal somethin' bluesy, Black man. I needs it too bad."

He could not refuse her. What came to mind was Billie Holiday's rendition of "Ain't Nobody's Business."

Well, I'd rather my man would hit me
than for him to jump up and quit me
Ain't nobody's business if I do
I swear I won't call no coppa, if I'm beat up by
my papa
Ain't nobody's business if I do, nobody's
business...

Instead, Eggplant Man sang Sam Cooke's rendition of

"A Change is Gonna Come."

I was born by the river in a little tent
Oh and just like the river I've been running
ever since
It's been a long, a long time coming
But I know a change gonna come, oh yes it
will
It's been too hard living but I'm afraid
to die…

As Eggplant Man skillfully plucked the soothing strings of his banjo, his mother's voice floated into his head. Mama had always said, "Boy, you never hits a woman, you hear me? If a woman make you mad, and they does, jus' walk away. Tha's what a real man do, you hear me boy? Amen."

"Yes Ma'am, Amen," he replied.

His father would just strum that banjo and be silent when Mama made him feel crazy or angry. He didn't walk away. He didn't raise his voice, but you could hear his banjo screaming.

Eggplant Man felt embarrassed looking at this woman's swollen face. The man who'd done this to her must not have had anywhere to walk or any song to play.

After he strummed and sang the final notes to Sam Cooke's song, there were fresh tears on the woman's cheeks. "Tha's what I'm talkin' 'bout, ...needed it, got it," the woman sputtered though her split lower lip. She dropped a dollar into his banjo case and walked back into her bruised life.

CHAPTER 15

....

Fear is stronger than Love, n'est-ce pas?

Stop turn around and look at me
Stop turn around tell me what you see
Is it love, is it real, can you deal with me?

Ruby saw Eggplant Man turn to look in her direction. He seemed to be playing his guitar. She wasn't sure if he was looking at her or just staring blindly ahead. She turned her glance downward.

Ruby did not know what to do. The warm syrup drizzle had now coursed its way through the narrow cleavage between her breasts, down the smooth road of her soft rounded abdomen. It finally reached the mound which overlooked a private world she had not visited in 20 years. She could barely breathe. Her inhalations were shallow incantations for mercy from a God. She had nearly forgotten and never forgiven God for the untimely atrocity of the loss of her mother and brother. Her exhalations were imperceptible efforts to release the bolus of air now stuck in the back of her throat.

She could hear Ma' Dear's voice from somewhere inside of her. "They love you and leave you, Baby. They don't never stay. It is damn hard to find you a good man unless you just plain lucky or 'specially blessed. And you ain't neither, you hear me Baby?"

"Yes. Ma' Dear," Ruby replied.

Her mother's warning about men kept whispering in her ear. In that moment, Ruby turned abruptly and headed back to her respite. She had to think. She needed to burn some candles. The smell of dark chocolate, tobacco and cloves wafted through her brain, smothering her. It was impossible to capture a deep breath. She felt a tingle course down the length of her scar. There was something pulling her to turn around and go to him, but her fear was stronger.

She found herself running past people who were just starting their own days. Ruby arrived at her abode. Pulling back the metal window cover too quickly, she slid into her space. The metal caught her arm, inflicting a superficial laceration as the plate scraped against her and then slammed shut. The sharp pain was a welcome jolt, giving her a moment to change her focus.

She felt warm blood ooze from the wound and run down her arm, matching the speed and consistency of the syrup river still coursing down the center of her body.

The blood had soiled her white tee shirt. Ruby pulled off the tee, wet the clean end from the thin stream of water constantly running from the bathroom shower and used her special bar of brown soap. She vigorously rubbed it against the wet shirt. She cleaned the wound, rinsed it and applied pressure until the oozing stopped. Then she lit one unscented candle.

Patiently, she waited until a small pool of melted wax formed around the wick. She adeptly applied the warm melted wax over the length of the wound until it dried and formed a neat bandage.

She felt trapped in her clothes, which were now wet with sweat. Ruby stripped completely. When she had removed her tee-shirt, a smell of fear blended with sensuality was released into the stagnant air of her apartment. As she peeled off her damp underwear, Ruby noticed the crotch of her white cotton panties. It was again filled with a creamy sticky discharge. Her right hand went nervously to her vagina, where she could feel a bean-sized bulge poking its way through the lips, boldly contacting the pad of her second finger. A pulsating surge of sensation moved out in concentric waves over her entire body. Ruby instinctively brought her index finger to her nose. Her own intimate odor was intoxicating to her. "Mercy, mercy!" Ruby called out, just in case God existed and was listening.

Feeling herself moving out of her domain of control, she quickly pulled out two more candles and lit them, watching all three flames dance and flicker. The candle fire competed the morning sun, which seeped into the room over the wood covering the window across the room.

Her mind drifted back to her morning encounter. She had run away! Ma' Dear's voice crept into her head. "Baby, runnin' away don't solve no problems. You gots to face it, and try yo' best to solve it or it follows you all yo' days. Baby, there ain't no place to hide from yo'self."

"Yes, Ma' Dear."

She could not imagine what Eggplant Man must think. Had he even seen her? Ruby's mind was racing. She had too many thoughts running around in her head. It was making her lightheaded.

She found her little plastic bag, two inches by two inches. It contained five miniature dolls made of cloth. Her mother, both a religious and a superstitious woman, had given her these little figures when she reached the age of reason, seven years old.

Ma' Dear had told her there would be times in life when she had to make important decisions. If she put the dolls under her pillow and slept on them, she'd been told, they would help her make good decisions while she slept.

"Only use these dolls for really important decisions, Baby," Ma' Dear had warned. "They is very powerful. If you misuse them they can drive you crazy."

"Yes, Ma' Dear," Ruby had replied.

To date, she had used them only once before, afraid of their power. She had slept with the dolls under her pillow when she was trying to decide whether to leave Metairie and move to New York. She had been expecting her good fortune ever since.

Her brain was tired, so Ruby decided to take a short nap. For a moment, she sat on her cot, nude and damp, her index finger resting under her nose. She inhaled the forbidden scent of her own desire, laid down in a fetal position and pulled some newspapers over her body. Placing the figurines neatly under her makeshift pillow, Ruby read the headline on her newspaper coverlet: "Woman Awakes From Coma" After 20 Years." The story wasn't important, she thought. It was all in the headlines. At that moment, she drifted into sleep.

CHAPTER 17
The First Wait

Baby, baby you're avoiding me
Don't you know what will be will be
The future knows as it takes its wind
A truer love you will never find

Eggplant Man was busy in his own thought processes. He was starting to get hungry. It crossed his mind that if he left, Ruby might return to find him gone. That he even had that thought scared and annoyed him. He could not let this thing mess with him. Rising quickly, he casually walked towards Amsterdam to the fast food stand and ordered a sausage sandwich and a coffee for $2.69. He purposely stayed there to finish it, chewing slowly, determined not to rush back to his spot. One of his mother's favorite dishes to prepare for the family breakfast was pork sausage smothered in onions, peppers and garlic, home-fried red potatoes, eggs easy over and buttermilk biscuits. His sausage sandwich meal was a far cry from how things used to be.

Back at Bubba's, Eggplant Man resumed his wall-holding position and closed his eyes. He began to reminisce about his childhood. He was trying not to think about Ruby. The strong sensation of heat and firmness in his groin was betraying him. His hands instinctively covered his aroused member, while the smell of coconut and honeydew filled his nostrils. His last thought before sleep was of his mother making biscuits and placing them in the wood burning oven. Eggplant Man was fading into a restless slumber.

Involuntarily, two words slipped from his lips: "Mercy, please."

CHAPTER 18

Night Magic in the Harlem's Summer

Ruby awoke to find that day had faded into evening. She could not believe she had slept so long. The candles had burned all the way down to their wicks with occasional alternating flickers of light remaining. She sat straight up with a startle, scattering everywhere the newspapers that had covered her. She detected the familiar sound of a rat scurrying across the floor towards the kitchen. Her abrupt awakening had obviously surprised it.

Her first thoughts were of Eggplant Man. He surely must have thought she was crazy, if he had even seen her at all. "Was he still there? she wondered. Where did he go at night, or did he sit there all evening? Most businesses didn't allow sleeping at their entrances at night. The white owners displaced from their uptown residences in New Rochelle or across the bridge in Queens, and the Asian owners with heavy broken English accents, were always adamant about their business entrances. Both groups had their harsh, condescending commands and threats.

Ruby had observed over the years that the Street Peeps—her own name for the homeless—sometimes sought shelter in the winter at the missions on Lenox and 114th or further downtown if available. Normally they were unsuccessful, as homelessness was rampant in Harlem in the 1980s and 1990s. Shelters were usually full, with long waiting lines by midday. The old and the disabled were often too slow, or unable to climb the steps to get to the sleeping quarters. Unable to fend for themselves, they were often the victims of crimes by other street people. No one ever seemed to pay attention to them. Some of the homeless even walked to the Bronx or crossed the 59th Street bridge to Queens, hoping to find temporary relief from the ravages of the city. Most of the street peeps just slept on the streets. They made use of doorways, store fronts, alleys or hallways of abandoned buildings overrun by drug addicts. In the hot and humid Harlem summers, many of the homeless just remained on the streets. In the winter, it was wicked. The weak often did not make it to the summer months. Ruby felt extremely lucky. She had her secret abode. This caused her to be overly diligent in changing her route home on a regular basis.

For a moment, she allowed her mind to entertain the fantasy of inviting Eggplant Man into her space for a night. The thought caused her to break out into a profuse musky sweat. The now familiar river of thick molasses began again its slow sensual journey between the cleavage of her breasts down a winding path, downward, downward. Ruby arose and ran into the bathroom, allowing the thin stream of cool water from the constantly flowing shower to chase the syrup, catch it and cool her down. Ruby quickly washed her body with the unscented soap and simply rinsed her face in the narrow stream draining from the rusty showerhead. Methodically, she got dressed, putting on a clean white tee and khakis. Remembering her arm laceration, she gingerly peeled off the wax covering. There was no pain or bleeding, but it was still a bit raw. Using the last of the melted wax on the bottom of the three candles, Ruby applied a new wax bandage to her wound. She then completely extinguished the candles. The room lit by moonbeams seeping eerily into her space.

"It must be about nine in the evening she thought. The moon was full. A good omen. Ruby felt. She unplaited her hair and brushed the 113 mandatory strokes to complete the mojo. She then applied her coconut oil and re-plaited her hair.

Pulling back her pillow, she viewed her five little problem solvers still lying in a horizontal line. Was her mind playing tricks on her? Had the doll in the red dress now moved to position number one, instead of position number two? Ruby sat on the cot and lit a candle momentarily to check it out. No, they were all in the same sequence. After she had reassured herself, Ruby blew out the candle and sat quietly in the moonlit darkness.

When night was approaching, she always sought the

security of her respite. As a young homeless female, Ruby had endured multiple verbal and physical assaults and harassments, when she first became homeless. It had become her policy not to roam the night streets of Harlem.

Now, however, she was feeling an insistent pull to return to 125th and Amsterdam. Ruby knew there would be many people out tonight. It was still hot and muggy and most people would find it difficult to sleep. In their crowded apartments, fans uselessly circulated stagnant heavy air. Blended scents of sweaty bodies, cooking grease, roach spray, cigarettes, dried urine and cheap cologne floated in the thick dampness. It hung like a dense nighttime cloud, ensnaring all of those beneath it to inhale its poison. Apartment dwellers and street peeps alike mixed together in the noxious heat. They joined together in some partner-less dance, each group boogying to its own music, sharing the same dance floor but imagining virtual detachment from each other.

Ruby slipped out into the alleyway, careful not to reinjure her arm. She looked up and down the length of the dark pathway and saw only several overturned trash cans with two hungry felines scavenging for food. She eased onto 114th Street, merged into the night culture and began her erratic walk up to 125th.

CHAPTER 19

Restless

Eggplant Man was so restless he could not sleep. The smothering New York humidity engulfed him, its weighted air forcing lots of people out into the streets. They arrived loud, boisterous and agitated from their inauspicious lives and the toxic hellholes in which they existed.

Eggplant Man wanted to escape the noisy crowd. Needing to clear his mind, he decided to strum a tune on his banjo. He suppressed a vision of Ruby's face that was straining to materialize in his mind. Usually, Eggplant Man found respite in his strings. To his dismay, his fingers, uninstructed, choose a melody that betrayed him. The mirage of Ruby's visage finally managed to emerge.

From nowhere through a caravan
Around the campfire light
A lovely woman in motion
With hair as dark as night
Her eyes were like that of a cat in the dark
That hypnotized me with love
She was a gypsy woman...

His fingers continued their involuntary strum.

Despite his inner protest, the 1970s Curtis Mayfield erotic hit, "Gypsy Woman," would not stop swimming in his mind. After his phalanges had finished their mutiny, He placed the banjo back into its case, locked it with a punishing snap and abruptly rose to find somewhere to sleep. Looking down 125th towards Amsterdam, he saw her standing there. Her familiar slight figure was staring back at him.

"There is a God after all," he thought, flabbergasted. "Sweet Jesus."

Eggplant Man began to walk slowly towards Ruby.

CHAPTER 20

Entanglement ... The Web We Weave

Ruby was frozen in place despite the city swelter. Her legs felt leaded, glued to the cement. The river of sweet nectar cruising down her body had finally crossed over Mount Pubis and was flowing through the crevice between her legs. It felt hotter than the heat of the night. Ruby feared it would continue its flow down her legs and drip embarrassingly onto the ground. It must have found its mark, however, because it stayed warm and sticky right where it was.

She saw him walking toward her. He was a big man, with broad shoulders, slightly bowed legs and mixed gray and black hair that defiantly stood four inches vertical on top of his head. Ruby noted he had high cheek bones, a strong nose, and that his dark purple skin was shining blue black in nighttime Harlem. His visage was hypnotic. He was looking dead ahead, directly at her.

Ruby's heart pounded uncontrollably against her chest wall. In moments, Eggplant Man stood directly in front of her, his six foot plus frame towering more than a foot above hers. He glanced down, patiently waiting for Ruby to make eye contact. Taking her hand into his, he exerted a reassuring squeeze. Ruby looked up but said nothing. Although she was silent, a single word screamed in her head: "Yes!"

With his money burning a hole in his sock, Eggplant Man had waited all day to ask one question: "Hungry?" He was yearning to do something for her.

Ruby replied with a subdued "Yes." She had not eaten in the last 24 hours, but eating was the last thing on her mind. She was much more aware of him holding her hand, causing her throbbing heart to jolt and her knees to quiver.

On 125th and Amsterdam, there was a coffee shop that stayed open 24/7 and didn't mind serving the homeless as long as they paid. The pair sat there for five hours sharing their stories, eating soup, sandwiches and drinking coffee.

Eggplant Man told Ruby his name was LeRoy but he liked the name she had given him. He explained that he, too, was from Metairie and remembered her story about the fire and her husband. He had wondered over the years what had become of her. Ruby did not remember crossing paths with Eggplant Man at all. It all seemed so natural between the two of them. It felt as if they were old friends. As dawn broke, a peacefulness came with it. Their glances and smiles grew longer, deeper.

Eggplant Man took her left hand into both of his and firmly massaged the palm. He was momentarily distracted when he noticed the tall brown-skinned lady again, dressed in shades of blue. She glanced casually at the engaged duo as she continued her saunter. He swiftly returned his attention to Ruby and looked profoundly into her eyes, searching for an answer to the question he really wanted to ask but did not.

"Where do you go at night, Ruby?" he asked instead. Ruby had never told anyone where she stayed. Her mother's warnings in reference to men rolled through her mind.

"Men love you and leave you, Baby. People die and men leave."

"Once they get it, they gone, baby."

"You lucky if they stays, and you ain't the lucky type."

"A good man is hard to find."

Ruby was hesitant, but she answered. "I stay on 114th Street."

As if he could read her mind, Eggplant Man whispered in a low tenor tone. "Don't worry, Ruby. I got you."

With that assurance, Ruby allowed him to walk home with her. She could not get past those three words. The "I got you" meant she was safe.

They turned into the alley between 115th and 114th Streets. Meandering down the dark pathway, strewn with garbage and debris, the pair arrived at the entrance to her dwelling. The cats were still there, now satiated and sleeping near the trash cans they had overturned.

Eggplant Man became acutely aware of the dangers Ruby faced coming to this place every evening. His mind was already thinking of ways to make it safer for her. Ruby pointed to her window entry. It was obvious Eggplant Man would not be able to easily slip in, as she had all of these years. He removed his jacket and rolled up his sleeves. He had to partially remove the metal plate and force it back, bending it to an almost 90 degree angle. Ruby watched his muscles flex as he forced the metal plate back. Once in, he adjusted the metal from the inside.

Ruby lit a large candle and placed it on the desk. She was nervous but excited. The molasses river which was latent in the crevice between her legs came alive now, and was bubbling. It sent pulsating waves beyond its borders. The throbbing sensation coursed back and forth in an undulating pattern, from the crack of her butt to the crannies of her labia.

Ruby craved for his touch, all over, especially where she throbbed. It amazed her that she was also aching to touch Eggplant Man. Her mother's advice on touching took a back seat to what she now felt.

Eggplant Man was as hard as steel. He felt the firm throbbing of his erect member and was trying to mentally offset the untimely conclusion to its rigid state. For a moment they stood facing each other, candlelight flickering. His dark eyes enveloped hers. Confidently, he pulled her to him, cupped her firm but quivering buttocks with both of his calloused hands and gently squeezed as his mouth found her erect nipples.

Eggplant Man's ebony lips then found Ruby's now

dancing scar. He gently planted multiple tender kisses along its length. The frolicking scar stopped its gyrations, enchanted by this new sensation. It submitted to the cleansing. The memory of what had happened vanished, as this new feeling replaced the old pain with pleasure.

Feeling the stark stiffness in Eggplant Man's groin, Ruby surrendered in an earthy moan. He deftly removed her clothes. Less skilled, she found it easier than she thought to undress this large man. Ruby succumbed and touched him everywhere. She kissed him wherever he was taut until he groaned. Nothing was out of bounds.

It was all smoky wine and dark chocolate, as they rubbed, caressed, weaved, entered private caches and imbibed each other's nectars.

At the end of their passionate embraces, they laid spent and exhausted, intertwined in each other's arms and lives. They were sprawled on top of Ruby's cot, with Eggplant Man's long legs and arms dangling languidly over the sides and Ruby curled up on top of him, in her usual fetal position.

CHAPTER 21
Love's Aftermath

Ruby awoke languorously around noon the next day. This was contrary to her normal 6 AM rising. Eggplant Man was still soundly asleep. The sun was at its brightest. Its rays were streaming into the room, over the tops of the wood plank and readjusted metal plate.

She took this opportunity to observe him unnoticed. Half of his body was hanging off her cot. His form was long, lean, and muscular, like that of a dancer. The sunlight caressing his skin cast vertical beams onto his naked, somnolent figure. It revealed that his entire body was covered with a flawless indigo pigment, matching his facial tone. The coarse silver strands infiltrating the black coils of his unruly hair glistened wherever they caught the sunlight.

Ruby felt a moment of tranquility, something she had never felt before. Ma' Dear's voice was just a whisper in her ear. "People die and men leave, Baby." Ruby could not manage a "Yes, Ma' Dear" this time. She could not imagine either of the two options.

The calm she had felt upon waking was ephemeral, as anxiety edged its way into her mind. Her scar began to twitch. Ruby stood under the cool stream flowing from the shower faucet. She positioned herself so that the water ran down the center of her body, creating erotic sensations in her pelvis. Anywhere she touched gave her small electric pulses. It forced her to think about the amorous events of the preceding hours. She was taken aback by the intensity of pleasure she was now feeling.

Ruby tried to dissipate these sensations by giving herself a thorough brown soap scrubbing. She pulled on her uniform of khakis and white tee, brushed her hair the mandatory 113 strokes, applied coconut oil and re-plaited the two braids.

Eggplant Man stirred with his subconscious brain recognition of the sweet-smelling oil. Not knowing what to say, she did not attempt to wake him. She slipped out of the apartment into the alley. Ruby needed to go for a walk and clear her head. It was Saturday and there was no garbage pick-up. Her plan was to stop by the mission on 119th Street to pick up some more soap, candles, toilet paper and tee shirts. It was part of the Daddy Grace legacy. Ruby would have remained helpless on the streets if it were not for the generosity of Daddy Grace and his followers.

She headed uptown toward the mission. The line was long this Saturday morning and it took more than two hours of waiting until her turn came.

She gathered the items for which she had come. Today they also had fresh fruit. Her favorite fruits, peaches and apples were in the selections. The red peaches, looking very juicy, enticed her. She took two peaches—one for Eggplant Man—and two apples for the same reason. Ruby then headed back uptown to her abode and back to her new man and new life paradigm.

She could feel some advice from Ma' Dear trying to push through. She had been suppressing her mother's whisperings since she had headed for her place last night with Eggplant Man.

"Baby, never let no man be yo' *raison d'etre*." It was not unusual for her mother, a Creole, to use French phrases in her conversations. "Fo' sure, they gonna disappoint you, Baby." Ruby knew it was too late for her to hold Eggplant Man in that regard. Her soul was already engaged. She was entangled.

CHAPTER 22

Dream Interrupted

Eggplant Man woke up about one half hour after Ruby left. He reached around in the haziness of just having opened his eyes in a dimly lit room. He needed to feel her soft skin under his rough fingertips, to make sure it was real. However, there was no Ruby to touch. Her fragrance still dangled in the air. He began to reminisce over the night's sweet encounter. His plan was to take Ruby to get something to eat and then to just spend the day with her, sitting in Central Park and getting to know her even better.

As his eyes adjusted to the darkness, he surveyed Ruby's place. "So this is where she escapes to each day," he thought out loud. It was a gloomy cache. There was an orderly stack of candles on the floor arranged by size and color, a makeshift cardboard box dresser containing folded white tee shirts, bras and panties. There were piles of tidily stacked newspapers on one side of a desk, and three large bottles of water lined up against the wall. There was a hair brush and a bottle of coconut oil placed next to the stack of papers. A few personal items also lay on the desk. These things represented her sparse life, nothing in excess, just the bare minimum. The only light entering the space came from the narrow beams of sunlight that streamed in through the cracks above the wood and steel plates over the windows. Eggplant Man contemplated that this was much more than he owned. All he had were the clothes on his back and his banjo. It was his banjo that saved him. For Ruby, he surmised it was her secret abode that saved her.

Guessing Ruby had gone for a walk, Eggplant Man decided he would go out to get some coffee and bagels for them. He wanted to take Ruby to Central Park and play a song he had created for her. His socks were not easily located on the floor. Finding them, he felt his left sock for the money he had placed there. Three dollars and change were left over from last night's meal. "We'll have to share the bagel," he mused.

Eggplant Man rinsed off in the thin stream of trickling water from the corroded shower head. He used Ruby's brown soap and could still detect her scent lingering in the bar. Afterwards, he quickly got dressed. All the while he kept having flashbacks of moments with Ruby. He had not been intimate with a woman for years. He was aware his member was now in full salute and he ached for Ruby again. In the past, whenever he had sexual urges, he would strum on his banjo and hum a bluesy refrain or satisfy himself in various dark alleys afforded by Harlem's streets. Now there was actually a being to desire. It all seemed surreal to him. Had the God his mother always talked about finally decided to shine light in his direction?

Ruby was definitely the woman for him. He'd felt it the moment he had touched her hand, when she gave him the vegetable skin. Or was it when he first saw her wounded eyes staring back at him from the Metairie newspaper years ago? Their lovemaking was a profound prayer. Their feral moans were primal. It was a calling out to each other from their cores. The groans uttered were a pleading to their souls to return to their abdicated thrones. In the midst of the passion, possibilities were overflowing. Promise lingered in the air...a hope for creation of an alternate paradigm, an option, a chance at a new life.

Eggplant Man eyed his banjo leaning upright against the desk. He had passed it to Ruby before he himself had entered through the window. It was begging him to be played. He decided to wait until they were in the park.

He grasped his banjo, stepped up onto the desk and exited Ruby's apartment. He replaced the steel plate so that she could re-enter without difficulty. He headed uptown to get the coffee and bagel. When he arrived at Amsterdam Avenue, he looked up and down the streets to see if he could catch sight of Ruby, but he did not see her.

Eggplant Man was in a happy daze. Thoughts of Ruby were swirling in his head. He was open to wherever this new relationship would lead him. He felt full of purpose for the first time since he left Metairie. He hardly noticed the familiar lady in blue heading towards him down Amsterdam. She looked intent on saying something to him this time.

Trying not to allow other thoughts into his head, he stepped off the curb of 125th and Amsterdam and was immediately hit head on by a yellow cab heading downtown. The last thought he had was of Ruby as he heard the sound of screeching tires.

The Saturday afternoon Harlem inhabitants and looky-loo's rapidly surrounded the fallen man. The cab driver was busy shouting obscenities about the homeless and explaining how he was not at fault. Sirens could be heard in the near distance making their way through busy Saturday afternoon traffic.

When the ambulance arrived, the crowd parted, allowing the medics to assess the crumpled figure for signs of salvage ability. They applied a neck splint and stabilized the spine of the unconscious man, lifted him onto a stretcher and loaded him into the back of the ambulance. Just as they were about to close the ambulance door, a tall stranger dressed in a cream linen suit, with a Stetson hat and brown and white Spectator shoes, picked up Eggplant Man's undamaged banjo and handed it to the attendant.

"He plays a mean banjo," the man informed the medic. The apathetic attendant reluctantly took the instrument. As the ambulance sped off to Harlem Hospital on 135th and Lenox Ave., the lady dressed all in blue with a matching hat and shoes shook her head in disbelief and pulled out her cigarettes. All that remained on the street was a large pool of blood already congealing in the Harlem heat, attracting many flies and displaying skid marks from the offending taxi.

CHAPTER 23

Mama Said There'd Be Days Like This

Ruby returned to her place after almost three hours. She was nervous and excited about seeing Eggplant Man. Should she start to call him LeRoy now? She could not wait to look into his eyes and to feel his reassuring arms around her. Her scar was now in motion, gyrating and tingling. He would calm it down for her, she anticipated. The metal plate had been repositioned and she noticed an almost hidden latch was in place behind the plate. Ruby knew Eggplant Man had fashioned this to make it safer and to facilitate her exit and entry. As she opened the plate, she slid her candles, teas, soap and fruit in first. In the heat of the afternoon she could smell Eggplant Man's scent lingering in the air. Her excitement was all encompassing. Her secret molasses river of heat had reached its mark a block before she arrived at her domicile.

Once inside, she saw no one. The emptiness was palpable.

Perhaps he had gone to get something to eat? Ruby noted his banjo was gone. She was angry at herself for taking so long to return. Why had she not wakened him before she left? Did he go back to Bubba's to play his Banjo? Ruby had an ominous feeling. It scared her.

She waited three more hours for Eggplant Man's return. She decided to walk to 125th and Amsterdam and see if he were sitting in front of the barbershop. The walk was long and she felt the force of gravity with each step. Her heart was pounding, her mouth dry and her chest heavy. Ruby was one block away and she was struck with the fear of what to say when she encountered him.

Her mother's whispers turned into screams, a cacophony of warnings and advice crowding her brain. "Slam bam thank you ma'am, men leave and people die, a good man is hard to find, why buy the cow when the milk is free, turn 'em upside down and they're all the same, they'll love you then you leave you lonely."

At the corner of 125th and Amsterdam. Ruby looked down the block and saw the empty space in front of Bubba's. She stood on that corner for two hours, afraid to move, to miss him.

The lady in sky blue sat on the porch steps of the corner apartment building, a brownstone in need of much renovation. She was watching Ruby, almost studying her, as she blew perfect circles of smoke from her cigarette. Ruby's hazel eyes were in full nystagmus now. Night was beginning to fall. Discouraged, Ruby headed back to her place.

The lady in blue took a long nostalgic drag on her cigarette, then put it out, smashing it punitively into the step. Ruby had a last hope that Eggplant Man might be in her apartment waiting for her. When she entered her dusky room, his aroma was still there. It hung stale and unpromising in the humid air. Ma' Dear was right after all. Ruby murmured in a whispered, defeated voice, "Yes, Ma' Dear."

CHAPTER 24
Staying Alive

Eggplant Man arrived at Harlem Hospital's emergency room in critical condition. He endured a basilar and parietal skull fracture with both blood and cerebral spinal fluid dripping from his fractured nose. There was a small bleed into the subdural area of his brain. He had a fracture at his fourth thoracic vertebrae, multiple rib fractures, one of which had punctured his lung. He could take only shallow, labored breaths, due to both a pneumothorax and hemothorax. Having sustained a displaced femur fracture, his right upper leg was grossly distorted, and swollen. His entire body was covered with multiple lacerations, abrasions and contusions. He had a brain concussion and remained unconscious.

After multiple units of blood and surgery to repair his fractures, he was admitted to the Intensive Care Unit. For five days, he remained in a coma. It was touch and go and his condition was listed as critical. They had shaved his head in order to take care of his head wounds. His crown of tightly coiled silver and black strands had fallen unceremoniously to the hospital floor. With no identification on his person, Eggplant Man was listed as a John Doe. He had lost so much blood the doctors were not sure he would survive the first 72 hours after admission, or if he would ever fully recover. The brain damage was mainly to the speech, memory and language processing areas. The swelling in his brain would take time to resolve. Yet he was alive!

CHAPTER 25

Remains of the Day

In her apartment, Ruby walked around in circles. Where a few hours earlier there had been ecstasy, all that remained was paralyzing fear and emotional devastation. What if Eggplant Man had abandoned her? How could she find him? Her routine garbage salvaging tours limited her to a set radius she had established 20 years ago. It would not allow her to venture too far north from 125th or south of 114th Street, or more than three blocks east or west of Amsterdam.

In the short time they had spent together, she had shared her wounded and fragile soul with Eggplant Man. Ruby could sense her eyes jumping erratically. Her scar began to ache like a fresh bruise. She undressed and let her body stand under the stream of cool water leaving the rusty shower head. It was her second shower that day and it brought her no relief. When she left the shower, Ruby made no attempt to dry off or get dressed. Trapped by her feelings, she wanted nothing to touch her body. She decided to light two candles. She needed to gather her thoughts.

Candles always facilitated her attempts to focus on her feelings. Ruby observed the flames hop around each other like two unrequited lovers, communicating in a strange dance of defeat. Two briny channels of tears effortlessly coursed her cheeks. Her blemish singed as one rivulet traversed over it. Reaching her thirsting lips, the salty streams entered her parched mouth. Ruby remained entranced by the dancing candle fires. Without any forethought, Ruby extinguished the fantasized fiery couple. She allowed the warm wax to melt into her fingertips.

Under her pillow, which had remained on her cot despite the adventures of the early morning, her little dolls were all in disarray. She carefully arranged them into an orderly line, methodically placing the pillow on top. Ruby curled up into the familiar fetal position on her cot, finger to nose, and fell into a deep sleep.

CHAPTER 26

Healing Music

A full week passed before Eggplant Man showed any signs of rousing. He became agitated and had to be restrained for his own safety. He was in and out of consciousness, and was not clearly verbalizing anything. The exceptions were the moans and groans related to his level of discomfort. He was prescribed 'round the clock' pain medication which muted the groans and forced sleep.

In a cast from head to toe, Eggplant Man resembled a gigantic mummy with splashes of onyx peeping through the bandages here and there. Although he was able to breathe on his own, he remained on a ventilator, which sporadically kicked on just in case he forgot or was unable to breathe adequately. By day 10, his pneumothorax and hemothorax had almost completely resolved, but tubes were still hanging out of his chest.

Despite his injuries, Eggplant Man was recovering well. The medical staff at Harlem Hospital playfully referred to him as Big John, although his hospital chart read John Doe. The hospital's utilization department was already making plans for his transfer to an ancillary rehabilitation facility once Eggplant Man was off the critical list and his recovery was imminent. The plan was the probable transfer to Franklin Center for Rehabilitation and Nursing in Flushing, New York. It would be an extended rehabilitative process.

By day 12, he was taken off the critical list and moved out of the Intensive Care Unit. He had begun to open his eyes off and on. He would stare in bewilderment at the white ceilings, sliding curtains and metal trays and railings. Still in pain, his wincing served as a clue to the nursing staff that his pain medications were due. He had no idea where he was or why. He felt as if he were in a haze of muffled voices and blurred faces and odd beeps, rings and mechanical sounds. He found himself thinking of his mother's biscuits with butter and syrup, which made him realize he was hungry. Each morning at seven-thirty a group of physicians and nurses would make joint rounds on John Doe. All tubes were removed by the fourteenth day and Eggplant Man needed no further assistance with his breathing. He was able to remain in a sitting position for most of the day without excruciating pain. His diet was unrestricted at this point. One of the interns had explained that he had been hit by a taxi on Amsterdam Avenue about two weeks earlier, and that he had been in Harlem Hospital ever since.

The attending of the rounding physicians asked him

his name each morning. He had no response to the query. He understood the question but for some reason could not muster an answer. Eggplant Man had no recollection of the taxi event. He was aware, however, that the staff was calling him John and that was not his name. The third time someone called him John, he simply said, "LeRoy, LeRoy Vaughn Reed," in his characteristic deep tenor voice.

Over the next two weeks, his recovery was continually progressive. He was assisted with walking the corridors daily and he had physical therapy three times a week.

Three days before his scheduled transfer to the rehab center in Flushing, one of the nurses recalled he had been admitted with a musical instrument. It had been his only belonging, other than the clothes he wore. After rounds, she brought it to his bedside. Eggplant Man emitted a deep guffaw, followed by a rush of emotion. Tears of joy flowed down his face. He had forgotten his lifelong friend and companion. The nurse cautiously handed him the instrument. His large hand first wrapped around the neck of his banjo. His calloused fingers knowingly began to slide over the top tuning pegs, then gingerly over the nut and frets to the fifth tuning peg, resting there for several moments. They continued their descent down the neck and fingerboard all the way to the bridge and tail piece. Running his fingers over the head, he circled the rim several times. The familiarity led to multitude of déjà vu memories flowing non-stop. Faces and places swirled around in his head. He tried fervidly to sort them into a chronological order. It overwhelmed him. For hours, he held tightly to his banjo. It was his connection to all that was. The nurses were unable to pry the instrument from his grip. Feeling some compassion, they allowed Eggplant Man the pleasure of his companion.

His fingers effortlessly tuned the instrument and soon fell into their rightful places on the expectant strings. Melodic jazzy lullabies filled the room and the sound waves wafted down the corridor. The first was Chet Baker's *'Chetty's Lullaby'* followed by Miles Davis's *'Blue in Green'* from his album "Kind of Blue." The employees, visitors and medical staff, fortunate enough to be on the ward at that moment, slipped into a bluesy calm. After his rendition, and exhausted by the memory onslaught, Eggplant Man fell into a deep sleep, still clasping his banjo.

Chet Baker
Chetty's Lullaby

Che Veglierò,

Questa notteÿ solo per te,

Dolce bimbo ti dirò che presto tornerò,

Senza te,

Sento gelo nel mio cuor,

Cerco solo

L'illusione

Di averti qui con me...

(English Translation:

I will watch,

This nottey̆ just for you,

Sweet child will tell you that I will return soon,

Without you,

I feel cold in my heart,

I just try

The illusion

To have you here with me ...

CHAPTER 27

Moving On

Ruby was in a miasma of devastation and confusion for the first two weeks following Eggplant Man's disappearance. She attempted to stick to her routine of the past 20 years. Unable to sleep well, she would awake early, with dried salt stains fixed on her cheeks. She spent extra time under the cold single stream of water and punishingly scrubbed her private areas extra hard with her brown soap. Ruby would don her white tee and khaki pants uniform. She found herself unplaiting and re-plaiting her hair multiple times, often without the benefit of the coconut oil and the one hundred and thirteen strokes. Eventually she would slip out of her apartment, unavoidably noting the crude metal lock Eggplant Man had fashioned for her safety.

Each day, Ruby would head up to 125th and Amsterdam to start her routine garbage rounds. Her eyes were always peeled for any sign of Eggplant Man. When she arrived at 125th, Ruby would furtively peek eastward towards Bubba's

Parlor. The empty space would starkly glare back at her. Often, Ruby lost track of time, and spent hours standing on the corner just waiting. Sometimes she missed the gray garbage truck passing by. Unknown to Ruby, she was being observed.

Nearby, standing on the weathered brownstone porch, was the lady in blue. She was lazily taking long, pensive draws on her Virginia Slims' cigarette. After two weeks of her futile search and wait regimen, Ruby stopped looking for Eggplant Man. As time passed and Ruby became more disillusioned, her behavior became increasingly erratic. Her ambulation became more jolted and her mumblings to herself were more frequent and louder. Her eyes took on a more feral stare.

Ma' Dear's voice was crowding out any thoughts of her own. It was a cacophony of advice and warnings. Ruby could not turn off the switch. For the first time that she could recall, she started having pounding headaches. It felt as if her head would explode.

It had been a month since she had last seen Eggplant Man. Ruby had a sense that an important part of her was slipping away. There was a void somewhere deep inside of her. She could not pinpoint exactly where it was. Her head felt separated from her heart. There was an unbearable combination of ennui and dispirited concern. The virtual sign hanging from her heart read, "Vacancy." Her head was saying, "No room in the Inn." Her appetite was gone. Her gaunt look was evidence that she was not eating.

Ruby knew she had to end this agony or she would not survive. Her first action was to change her trash tour route to avoid passing 125th and Amsterdam. Since today was the thirty day anniversary of her romantic interlude with Eggplant Man, Ruby decided to make it her last time going back to Bubba's. She walked with leaded legs back to 125th. This time would be different. Ruby felt she would have closure by standing directly in front of the parlor and sitting on the spot where he had sat, for the past twenty years.

A cold sweat appeared on her forehead as she reached the structure. Her knees became shaky and Ruby could sense the molasses river starting to flow between her breasts. The Taiwanese owner wandered outside with his broom and began to sweep the area in front of his shop. He encountered Ruby standing there just staring at the ground. In a heavy accent, the man scowled, "You go 'way. You no stay here. Bad for business. Things betta' now tha' man gone. You go 'way." With his broom, he made a sweeping gesture towards Ruby.

She could not muster one word. She thought about the phrase the parlor shop owner had used, "tha' man gone." Ma' Dear's voice managed to slip through the myriad of warnings: "Men leave and people die."

She was still processing the thought of Eggplant Man's leaving her when she felt a presence behind her. She turned brusquely around. Ruby found herself eye to eye with the lady in blue. She was close enough for Ruby to smell her stale cigarette breath and cheap perfume. Unprompted, the lady asked and answered her own question in a raspy smoker's breath.

"You lookin' for the banjo man?" Her foul breath rested momentarily on Ruby's face, causing her scar to twitch. "Ambulance took him to Harlem Hospital after that taxi hit him, about a month ago. He was hurt real bad, though."

The shop owner, overhearing the conversation, chuckled and mumbled something under his breath, in his native tongue. He then went back into his shop.

Ruby was dumbfounded. The swirling in her head, combined with the knot in her stomach, caused nausea. She retched several times but it was unproductive. The cold sweat had now enveloped her body, in contrast to the hot syrup rivulet descending down her middle.

The lady in blue took a deep drag on her Virginia Slims fag, then brusquely walked away, with swirls of cigarette smoke in hot pursuit. She felt pleased after releasing the information she had held hostage for the past month.

Ruby headed uptown towards 135th and Lenox. Harlem Hospital had been the predominant health care facility in Harlem for many years, serving the economically disadvantaged community, primarily the African American population.

When Harlem Hospital Center opened its doors on April 18, 1887, it was located at the juncture of East 120th Street and the East River. The hospital was a former Victorian mansion. Prior to the 1900s, the Dutch-founded Harlem served a very different population of immigrants, primarily the Eastern Jewish and Italian populations. Soon southern African Americans and West Indians began to migrate to Harlem. By the 1920s and 1930s, the Harlem Renaissance was in full swing and Blacks in Harlem were flourishing. In 1907, Harlem Hospital relocated to its present location on 135th Street, and was therefore a facility well known to all Harlem residents.

When Ruby entered the huge hospital lobby, she was awestruck by boldly displayed murals which artfully showed the journey of African Americans throughout history. Ruby had never seen anything like this. Two murals, *Magic in Medicine* and *History of Medicine,* held her attention. She looked deeply into one of these Charles Alston masterpieces. One of the painted figures in *History of Medicine* strongly resembled Eggplant Man. The painted man had similar ebony-colored skin, flaring nostrils and a crown of coiled hair. She divined that he was a part of that painting, a part of that history. It was an auspicious occasion for her, a good omen. To her, it meant that Eggplant Man was all right.

She walked bravely to the front desk, but discovered she was unable to speak. She picked up the sign-in pen and a sheet from the adjacent hospital memo pad and wrote the name "Leroy Vaughn Reed" in large letters. She handed the paper to the clerk, who was already eyeing her suspiciously. The clerk had a rigid appearance, her hair tightly pulled into a severe bun slicked back with greasy pomade.

"Probably Dixie Peach or Royal Jelly," Ruby muttered to herself.

The woman's coif displayed an artificial wavy pattern, obviously achieved by sleeping with a tight nylon stocking on her head all night. No wonder she appeared irritable, Ruby thought. "She probably has a headache."

Meticulously, the clerk searched her file book marked "Inpatients." She was obviously apprehensive about Ruby. Several times, she furtively glanced up to look at her. After what seemed like an eternity to Ruby, she finally spewed a response, in a thick West Indian accent, "Nobody here wit' dat name." Her attitude was as stoic as her hair.

Ruby's scar started its nervous dance. The clerk was annoyed by the twitching lesion and Ruby's presence in general.

"There's no loiterin' allowed in dis' lobby," she snorted, with a meaningful glance in the direction of the security guard.

As Ruby quickly exited the lobby, a floor clerk arrived with the updated register of inpatients and the list of discharges scheduled for the day. The lobby clerk noted that the last name on the alphabetical list of discharges was a Leroy Vaughn Reed, aka John Doe. She looked up but Ruby was well on her way back to 125th Street.

Ruby's mind could not encompass the death of Eggplant Man. She stuffed the thought into her secret cerebral closet along with her mother and brother's death experience. Her plan was to discover a new garbage tour route for herself. Ruby needed closure.

She decided to make a final visit to Bubba's Parlor. She only wanted to sit where Eggplant Man had sat and played his banjo. Ruby needed to wallow in the memory for a short time and then have final closure to that phase of her life.

CHAPTER 28

Destiny's Restoration

Today was transfer day for Leroy. He had come a long way since the day he was admitted to ICU, a month ago. He knew he was being sent to a rehabilitation facility in Queens, called Franklin Rehabilitation Center, for another four to six weeks of therapy. He was able to ambulate with minimal pain and a moderate limp. Mentally he was still trying to place all the pieces of his life puzzle together. Many of his early life memories had returned fully. His musical recollection was outstanding. What his mind did not consciously recall, his experienced fingers remembered. The day surrounding his accident was still a blur. Sporadic flashbacks, with flickers here and there of faces and places, emerged involuntarily. The neurosurgeons said his very recent memories surrounding the accident might never return. There was a possibility, however, that an emotional event could trigger the return of his recall of events surrounding his accident. Only time would tell.

The hospital staff had become attached to Leroy and his music. It had changed the atmosphere of the ward in a wonderful way. Only music, the universal language, can do this. Leroy sat in his wheelchair with the Daddy Grace mission's donation clothes on his back. He was handed a plastic bag with the bloody torn clothes in which he arrived, and of course his banjo, his sole earthly possession.

His hair was starting to grow back. There was now a half inch thick gray and black tightly coiled corona on his head. All of the staff came over to shake his hand and wish him luck. One nurse bent over to plant a kiss on his cheek. In the process, she scraped her own cheek on the top of his banjo. A small amount of blood oozed from the scar. The nurse pulled out a tissue, dabbed at the lesion, and pulled out her compact mirror from her pocket.

"Don't worry," she said. "It's superficial, and it certainly won't leave a scar."

Leroy emitted a deep grunt and stared ahead blankly. A memory was trying to burst through. A flash of a woman with a scar on her cheek and piercing hazel eyes momentarily flickered and then disappeared. It was accompanied by a strong sensation in his groin. The unperceiving staff reassured him that the nurse's abrasion would heal fine. For the length of his elevator ride to the lobby he tried to relax his mind so that the emerging memory could fully express.

While he waited by the lobby clerk's reception desk for the transport team, Leroy was taken by the beautiful murals on the lobby's walls. He overheard the lobby clerk tell the ward clerk that some homeless lady with a horrible c-shaped scar on her cheek had been there earlier, looking for Mr. Vaughn. She released herself from blame by complaining that the floor clerk had not given her the updated patient list on time.

Immediately, Leroy was in motion. He stood up, banjo in hand, walked across the lobby and out the front door.

The two clerks called after him. "Mr. Leroy Vaughn Reed! Mr. Reed! You are leaving Against Medical Advice. You need to sign papers! Mr. Reed!" The clerk looked towards the security desk, but the guard was nowhere in sight.

Eggplant Man did not hear them. He was too busy with the memories rolling into his head. Once on the street, he knew exactly where he was. The fog was lifting. As he headed downtown towards 125th street, one word popped into his head: "Ruby."

He could not remember where she stayed. But he had full recall of her. Eggplant Man remembered exactly how Ruby smelled and tasted, and the feeling of her lips pressed against his. He was moving so fast he did not feel any pain in his leg. When he reached 125th Street and Amsterdam, he headed east. He opened the plastic bag with his old clothes, searched the left breast pocket of his jacket. The now dried eggplant skin was still there. Even dried, it retained its color and texture. His sock still had three dollars and change in it.

At first glance he did not see her; her slight figure was easy to miss. As Ruby slouched against the parlor wall, her head was hung low. She was watching a line of ants dutifully clean up the remains of some food item on the ground. She mused distractedly at the organized tiny creatures.

Deciding she had wallowed enough, she decided to go back to her place. She would burn two candles, as part of her makeshift ceremony of closure. When she stood up, she noticed a male figure limping towards her. She did not recognize him right off. He had lost a lot of weight, had no crown and was limping. Ruby's soul knew it was Eggplant Man.

When he arrived at the parlor, the two souls faced each other, staring into each other's eyes for a long time. As they embraced each other, tears streamed down their faces. Each could hear the other's heartbeat synchronized to the same rhythm.

Eggplant Man whispered softly in her ear, "Hungry?"

Ruby responded in a honeyed voice. "Very."

He confidently took her hand in his. "I got you, Ruby."

Ruby's eyes misted as her lips curved upwards, causing the scar on her cheek to tingle. Hand in hand, the couple headed toward the 24-hour deli on 125th Street.

From her porch, the lady in blue watched, blowing perfect circles of smoke.

END

Printed in the United States
By Bookmasters